WHAT THE SAND DIDN'T TELL THE MOON

ALSO BY RIC HOOL

Fitting In With Malcolm (WYSIWYG Chapbooks, 1994)
Making It (The Collective Press, 1998)
The Bridge (The Collective Press, 2000)
Voice from a Correspondent (The Collective Press, 2001)
No Nothing (The Collective Press, 2009)
Selected Poems (Red Squirrel Press, 2013)
A Way of Falling Upwards (Cinnamon Press, 2014)
Hut (Woodenhead Pamphlets, 2016)
Between So Many Words (Red Squirrel Press, 2016)
Personal Archaeology (Red Squirrel Press, 2020)
Containing Multitudes (One Hand Waving Press, 2022)
Since I Last Wrote (Red Squirrel Press, 2023)

What the Sand Didn't Tell the Moon

SHORT STORIES

Ric Hool

Postbox PRESS

First published in 2024 by Postbox Press,
the literary fiction imprint of Red Squirrel Press
36 Elphinstone Crescent
Biggar
South Lanarkshire
ML12 6GU
www.redsquirrelpress.com

Layout, design and typesetting by Gerry Cambridge
gerry.cambridge@btinternet.com

Cover image: Colin Burt & Tim Rossiter

Copyright © Ric Hool 2024

Ric Hool has asserted his right to be identified as the
author of this work in accordance with Section 77
of the Copyright, Designs and Patents Act 1988.

All rights reserved.

A CIP catalogue record for this book is available
from the British Library.

ISBN: 978 1 913632 61 8

Red Squirrel Press and Postbox Press are committed
to a sustainable future. This publication is printed in
the UK by Imprint Digital using Forest Stewardship
Council certified paper.
www.digital.imprint.co.uk

Contents

Two Types of Dog / 9
Breakfast in Alcover / 13
Desert Night / 17
Two Thirds of Granada / 27
The Holy Ground / 29
Crimson on White / 33
IOU / 39
Take it Handy / 43
Caña = A Glass of Beer / 47
A Wedding at Al Gorrobo / 51
DJ Hiatus / 53
Only a Tale / 57
August Fishermen / 61
Finding the Lost World / 63
Starting with a Fine Hat / 67
Post / 71
Fish / 75
The Blues / 79
Last Fair Deal Gone Down / 83

Acknowledgements / 91
A NOTE ON THE TYPE / 92

for Ian Brinton
siempre

Two Types of Dog

THE WALK BEGAN at the end of a flat concrete road that had been laid down bit by bit to service apartments and smallholdings as they sprouted upwards into scrub towards the hills. The buildings freckled the land either side of the single lane. There was even a tiny shop that sold everything from bobbins of cotton to cans of baked beans.

Dogs regularly barked aggressively, running out to the limits of their chains from buildings to front gates. Rough, unhappy dogs that knew no better.

A road like this runs away from people and civilization whilst pretending to do the opposite. It takes its poorly tamped-down concrete surface up to the beginnings of high ground.

At a point, as the land rises steeply, both the concrete and the buildings run out. The vigour of natural topography kicks in. The route swung to the right, dirt all the way up. To the left a driveway with a sign: PRIVATE ROAD.

The track rose steeply bending this way then that as a track does when making its way up a mountain. Trees to the left, down to a ravine, had been burned a short while ago and showed no green regrowth. To the right, trees and shrub were scorched by sun. The rough road pulled itself up as if it was stalking the blue sky above.

Heat got up, sucking moisture through skin leaving the body tracked in threads of water incising dust that thickened then caked muddy on wet flesh. Plants nearby grew twisted and cruel, spiked and barbed. A lizard, hard to distinguish from stone, didn't bother to scurry away. It clenched low to the ground, trapping its shadow.

On, on, up, up and higher the land sprung all around like the backbones of a nest of dinosaurs.

A tiny chapel almost at the top of the mountain was a target but was passed by as the summit beckoned only another fifty metres further and there, levelled out for ten or fifteen metres. The view shot north-east over faraway Skiathos Town, further across water and islets to Glossia on Skopelos and east to the bay of Platanias and Aghia Paraskevi. In the quiet moments, mopping up the panorama and listening to my slowly regulated breathing and with the sun's crepuscular light behind, the image of the Lady Columbia illuminating the world filled my mind.

A light touch on my right calf broke the moment without startling me. I was not alone. It was a small white dog with a long body, her face three dark spots like the grips on a bowling ball. Speaking gently in rag n bone Spanish (the best dog language I know) I reached down to stroke her muzzle then her ears, 'Enamorada, yo t'gusto. Ven aqui.' It did the trick. The little dog was happy to take my gentle strokes and did so without convulsing into fawning wriggles and I enjoyed her softness, her unexpected presence.

Standing upright and with my new-found friend leaning against my leg I returned to the view of headlands and islands, turquoise sea carefully poured into place, yellow smiling beaches and laughing orange groves, branding them into memory.

I turned to walk back down the mountain and made a friendly gesture to the dog, patting my thigh to encourage her to come with me. She would be good company on the way down and after all, must have wandered from somewhere off the concrete road at the bottom. But no, as friendly as she had been, what I did made her scoot off where she stared at me differently. There was no persuading her.

The trek down seemed lonelier. The landscape affected me less. The steep dirt track absorbed the drum of each step as puffs of dust exploded around each foot. The sun eclipsed behind ridges as I dug deeper, heading for the concrete road, a visible pale scar a way off.

I kept thinking of the small white dog. Why had she appeared at the top of my journey? Where had she come from? Why didn't she return with me?

After another hour I reached the concrete road, put one foot on it, and heard the unmistakable scrape of a long chain being dragged quickly over the ground, accompanied by snarling, growling, and barking.

Breakfast in Alcover

ANOTHER POSTCARD to write and yet another hot morning brands itself into the month. What to say? Describe the dead dryness of the land, its readiness to burst into flames? That happened two weeks ago on hills a few miles away. Now remnant blackness chars the horizon and worries vision. Everyone is twitchy. More so during daylight when it's not so easy to detect the start of a fire and when spirals of dust whipped up by traffic raise the tension. At night people stay up late or get up from time to time to check for tell-tale licks of light. Everyone is jumpy.

Thirty, I count them, incandescent bee-eaters are perched on the wire from the house away to the pole down by the road. They have made a dazzling necklace of that ordinary cable for the past two mornings. I haven't mentioned this to any of the locals in case it translates to a bad omen that heightens fears even more. Any other time I'd be told the bee-eaters birth from morning dew then sprout wings or some such wondrous tale. But people have been preoccupied of late. Anyway there is no dew.

Here comes the old man who sits every day in the shade of the small olive grove opposite, trapped within the road's bend before it zigzags up to the top and over the hard knuckled mountain. He never talks. He looks like the trees, short and tough. Most days a young woman, say, in her late twenties, I guess his granddaughter, arrives in a car with his lunch in a wicker basket but after a blazing row the other day she hasn't shown, nor has anyone else for that matter. What the row was about I don't know but it was loud from the woman. Spanish words like wasps buzzed from her mouth, she stamped back and fore, her arms raised like crooked aerials above her head. Every now and then she'd point across to my place which made me a little embarrassed, as if I shouldn't have been witnessing the fracas.

In the midst of the row a car screeched round the bend.

I've been here for almost six months, house-sitting. The owner needs to stay in his apartment at the coast, close to his tourist business interests. I say house-sitting but it's larger than most and, being in Spain, is a villa set in its own grounds above the small rural town of Alcover. Along with general house duties there is the garden to maintain and water, though with the drought water has been regulated.

Security is a low level affair, just letting passers-by see me about the place and having lights on at night. Part of my routine is to breakfast al fresco at the front hence my ringside seat to the blow up the other day. All in all, the job has a leisurely pace to it. Nice work if you can get it.

Back to the postcard.

I can précis the tale of The Huesca Bell...how a young, inexperienced king, torn from his life within a monastery and untrained in statesmanship, sought the advice of his old teacher in order to make sense of the bad decisions being made for him by the wise men of the court. How the old monk said nothing in reply but swept the head off each weed with his stick as he passed. How the inexperienced king understood his teacher and returned to his court to execute the advisors, one by one and hung each head with rope from the vaulted roof of his great hall. The heads dangled like grotesque clappers. The young king then led in his new advisors to see the fate of the last.

He received far better advice from the new team.

The card's white space is challenging, asking to be soiled by thought and action. Its two different sides are eyes of a single chameleon.

Breakfast is a caesura and feeds the starved night whilst suckling the born day.

These are big thoughts.

I wonder if the old man will turn up and if so, what will he eat for lunch?

Perhaps I will sit forever at breakfast in Alcover with this postcard in front of me, or once more discover the bee-eaters.

Desert Night

1. *History*

It was 1967 and things were wild in San Francisco. In England bare feet began walking the streets. Hair was long, entangled with flowers and a joint had nothing to do with Sunday roast. Everyone was making music. The *really* beautiful people were making music in hide-away cottages. Days and weeks swirled in sweet joss stick smoke, stirred by dreams of splitting for India and gently thrummed by the beat of tablas.

It was 1976 and Punk was in the street, cockroach-black and any plastic wrapped around the body was anti-establishment. Everything was stand up — lifestyles, comedy, hair. A subculture of subterranean youth snarled, curled its lip and clumped its heavy feet over the ashes of hippiedom.

The summer of '76 cooked the British like fresh shrimps, melted roads and ice-cream had no chance. The rear-guard of would-be Haight-Ashbury copyists turned on and tuned in to the heat and let it breeze around them as they dressed in new stocks of Indian wear from a whole new chain of shops supporting a new generation of British Asians.

Things were getting 'ethnic' and freedom played its simple tune once more.

It was 1988 and the dream pinched hard on his bum after twenty-four hours of driving. There had been only one brief stop for petrol and a coffee.

Freedom had quit playing her whispering game, had ceased to surround herself with good sense, had hitched up her full skirt to the very top of her shapely thighs, tossed back her dark hair and said, 'Want me? Then come and get me!'

So there he was, down past France and into Spain.

2. *Escape*

France had been an overnight speedway of holiday traffic that jewelled the road south as far as looking allowed. The whole nation was out that night burning yellow headlights over the road. He felt alive to be part of this forever serpent of lights, twisting and turning ahead towards a point where half of the creature broke to veer east in the direction of Marseilles and the French Riviera. His route swung the other way, south and west beyond Orange and Arles, putting the rising sun to his side and back as the VW camper cruised past Aigue Mortes, its Camelot turrets and imprisoned princesses, along the lagoon-looped coastal hop from Le Cap d'Agde, past Sète, to La Grande-Motte, on a full southerly curl to the Spanish border.

The frontier, sparse and left over, was fraught with the usual irrational feeling that a criminal act was taking place. He observed the protocol, produced his passport and declared, 'Holiday.' The guard looked at the van's number plate then called out over his shoulder. Another customs officer, attended by a brown and white spaniel, came out of a flat-roofed building and signalled to vacate the vehicle.

At that time the full impact of running a Q registered camper smacked him dumb. The conversion of the VW into a smart camper had been done by a firm who imported commercial vans, then chopped the tops off and did a wonderful caravanning job, carpets, cooker, fridge, seating, beds and then re-registered the vehicle as British, legally, under Q plates. Trouble was he knew the van had come from Amsterdam. Sure, the dog would find something left over from that place, drugs, diamonds or both! For what seemed like an eternity the dog sniffed like a Dyson. The guards took panels off doors. The whole camper was emptied.

At a point when nerves had reached breaking point and the camper looked like a half-complete construction kit, the guard handed back his passport, dispassionately said, 'Anda!' and waved him through. He shoved things in quickly and drove.

Several miles down the road, past La Junquera, he pulled over to sort things out properly. Looking at the chaos behind the driver's seat, his mind flashed back to the border experience and its terrible possibilities. He shivered.

3. *Lady of the Night*

Eating, breathing, seeing, swimming in his new-found freedom, he discovered a dimension hardly known to him. *Being* took a brand-new hold on him. 'Hello!' he would say to strangers and mean it, instead of chucking the word out like discarded chip-wrapping. He smiled more; was surprised when catching his lit face reflected in a window. He listened to life detonate around him in a language the meaning of which sailed away in misunderstood laughter.

Nights were spent parked near lonely beaches, the camper's side door slid open welcoming the gentle tenor of a lazy tide, and the air, scented with the deep sweetness of *lady of the night*, was a sensual balm.

Each evening he would write poetry, put it in a plastic bag and bury it, making an exploratory trail of writing as he drove on. Who would find his poems?

Perhaps he would, in years to come, recoup them, one-by-one in the company of a lover in some absurdly romantic paper chase.

4. *The Magnificent Bird*

Crossing Puente del Diablo he saw a magnificent bird, feathers aflame in oranges and blues. By some magic it rolled itself into a ball, flew and rolled, flew and rolled, as if it had been thrown by a god.

He spread his elbows across the steering wheel, cupped his hands, awaiting a catch.

5. *A Nodding Acquaintance*

At Tarragona he flipped a coin between grabbing a boat

for the Canary Islands or a visit to the nearby Roman amphitheatre. The Romans won again.

In the warm calmness of that morning the theatre of treachery could not be assimilated. He walked its circle alone and sat several times at various vantage points and tried to imagine manifestations of its bloody past but without success. Instead he left taking with him the modernity of that toga totin' race and not least their contribution to twentieth century landscape. Next was shopping.

At a café he met a fat Irishman who ran a language school, and fell in love with his beautiful, swollen, Irish mind, the thoughts of which, like liquid, found themselves contained in whatever might hold a conversation. This was a magician under whose spell any person would fall. Truth was a yarn. To lie was a sin and to sin was an obligation. Anyway, Brendan Behan *had* decorated his father's flat and written the complete script of *The Quare Fellow* in pencil on the ceiling before covering it with whitewash. 'In fact,' the fat Irishman said, 'it was the standin at the topuv them laddrs an that platted loight cord, gave him the oidea... that an the room bein so bare, loike a cell.' The Irishman talked and storytold and recommended places to visit before rushing off, late for his class.

Early the next morning, taking the Irishman's advice, he drove away from the coast into the hills where 'the real Spanish people live' and soon was on a winding route up to the mountains behind the small village of Alcover. Just outside the village, in a bend of the road before it zigzagged up to the high ground, he saw an old Spanish man and a younger woman having an explosive argument in an olive grove. Opposite, outside a villa, another man was at a table eating breakfast, al fresco, witnessing the row. There seemed everything familiar yet virgin about the event.

The road didn't stop rising and twisting for the next six miles until it levelled out enough for a field or two to be cultivated next to a farmhouse-cum-bar, built into the jaws of an astonishing view that took the eye higher to saw-edged peaks and lower to ragged, derelict, land-slid valleys. There was nothing gentle about the countryside. Gnarled trees grew old from splintered rocks, roots forced through the smallest of fissures and wiry grasses skewered the air. Every plant snagged and tore clothing. Here was the unforgiving smell of dry earth. The quickening of loneliness drove him from that place.

For the next day the camper descended slowly on heated brakes until joining the coastal route where misanthropy was cloaked in commerce and the need to make a buck sustained a society he recognised. He had fun again, eating seafood and drinking small cold beers, often in bars loud with noise. In one bar with blaring music, he was swept into a dance and the rest of the evening with a woman with Debbie Harry cheekbones and red, pouted lips. Walls were blasted by music drummed and thrummed, beaten and brawled. So it went until the swollen night subsided into fragile moments of uncertainty when couples on scattered islands of tables grappled for words to sustain them further into the dawn. Tired bar staff surrounded a communal table; ate and shared tips.

Her name was Sun Child and she spoke of herself as if she wasn't there. Here is Sun Child's story, in her words.

I always wanted to catch the sun in bleached hills splashed with white houses, where orange stone slopes turned from the glare, and motes of dwellings reminded me of fungus mould on childhood goldfish. They had been my young suns rising and falling in their glass galaxy. I walked through Spanish streets trenched by tall houses before liberating myself to no man's land between village and hills, to a point where road crumbled to path then disintegrated to track. I had no jewel to brooch the interior and dressed in cream and khaki, though I had brought a green frock to wear during December rains. I was quite mad by then and measured myself, with arms angled, beside a slow growing cactus. I watched migrating birds fly south chasing the elusive sun.

One night, in a bar, I kissed a man then slept with him. I wore my green dress but bought a gold one. I met another man… another…

6. *A Song Composed in the Desert Night*

On a late afternoon when his mind and body were only vaguely in touch, he was driving the camper southwards on a long, straight, empty road with mountains running parallel to the right. From the lips of a crag that looked like Jim Morrison's face, he saw an eagle rise, carrying a book in its talons. Away the bird flew, higher and higher carried by thermals, accelerating the bird to a speck in the ever-deepening blue sky. He stopped the van, looked back but the light and perspective had changed, gone, along with Jim Morrison's face... as rapidly as that... as sudden as life.

That strange late afternoon took the camper many miles down that long empty road which he drove with one arm crooked out of the wound-down side window, his concentration divided between road and mountains. He took in how big the roadside hoardings were and how grand and regular was that cut-out black bull advertising brandy. With so few cars on the road the advertisements seemed wasted: as an art gallery, he had seen few better.

He began to understand the anxiety of open space, its lack of internal reference and why its punctuation satisfies the optic sense. Perhaps the eye never really sees space at all, only the detail held in it.

The road space in front of him darkened and narrowed ahead to a point where a little figure had an arm out and a thumb jerked in the way of hitchhikers. She was a small, beautiful woman. He smiled because she smiled so whitely and broadly against her brown-skinned face. There was no embarrassment and little conversation between her getting in and driving down the road until night closed around the camper, sucking on its headlights. After a few more miles he had to pull over onto the scrub desert that began an inch away from the roadside, and cash-in the day's driving.

The brown-skinned woman, who spoke very little and what little in an Andalucian dialect that severed word endings, ramming them into the next like a motorway pile-up, would have to hitch on through the dark or spend the night with him. 'Aquinopr'l'm,' she whispered without emotion and did something at the back of her head that made thick, brown hair collapse around her dusky-skinned face which melted against the night. He thought that moment the most beautiful and most unexpected in his entire life.

Without more being said, wood was collected and lit in a neat fire a small distance away from the open-slid side door of the VW. The inside of the camper glowed in the fire's mellow light. All was hushed but not silent as the night grew into an enormity of blackness, punctured by a million stars. Cooling rocks near and far cracked like pistol shots as temperature dropped. Shattered particles added to the desert's detritus. The susurration of insect wings orchestrated the blackness, and the wind began to sing itself around a wire above the road in a sad lullaby, as if from a late working mother to her restless child, fighting against sleep until her return home.

And so that song, sung in the desert night worked itself to an end, leaving its audience wondering if there would be a next time?

He looked at her across the fire-glow and thought how lovely she was and how beautifully she belonged to the desert night. If he ever had to tell anyone what beauty was, he would answer: *beauty is a dark-skinned Spanish girl, travelling through the desert, sitting at the roadside, her face lit by a campfire which throws its flamed hands up in applause to the desert night.*

Two Thirds of Granada

AROUND GRANADA the Sierra Nevada Mountains hike their peaks to the high air, sawn through by streams since planet Earth buckled its crust at that random spot during the New Fold epoch. He made a mental note of how fresh they looked compared to the Caledonian Mountains of Scotland which ached with age, waiting to be worn to peneplain like the ancient Laurentian Shield of Canada. The Highlands contained a deep and dark magic, these upstarts only beginning their journey.

In the Moorish city streets of Granada vendors sold pistachios, eaten whole by kids who spat out the shells — kids with fresh faces and gunfighter stares, their hair slicked back, early-Presley style. The same paladins made short shrift of succulent olives from fat barrels of brine, blowing the stones out of their mouths, making popping sounds like shots from muffled pistols.

He has three stories of Granada.

One is a night, after working *El Shakespeare*, into the early hours of the morning, his throat dry and sore after hours of singing, his fingers raw after hours of guitar playing. *Thank god I don't dance*, he thought. The night was so late a drink was hard to find in the closed-up city and when he did find a bar, he had to keep it open by drinking quickly then ordering another. This went on to its inevitable end when he found himself spewed up at a churro stand, his drunken pockets lightened by the first wave of shivering market workers.

Another story is a walk from one side of the city to the other along the seemingly never-ending main drag, underneath the high built flats of the well-heeled, past the vendors outside the low, brown tenements of the unknown, clustered like molluscs around communal front doors, jabbing each other with street talk. Over and over he would see them cut their backs to the uniformed police patrols and tiredly but loudly groan the word, *Mono*.

He guessed this did not approximate to anything like, *good evening officer*. These were the young cats, The Jets, The Warriors, Montagues and Capulets who kept the peace or else made war on the streets of Granada. The Young Turks smoked, drawing demon-hot points to their cigarettes and blew blue smoke past the weary gaze of yellow, ground floor apartment windows.

This is a story of a walk from one side of a city to the other where cars shook themselves out between traffic lights that captured them in screeched brakes and released them in revved-up engines coughing fumes into the hot, breathless air. All the way buildings clotted, humans curdled and the bacilli of cars spread, bursting into every offshoot road, their horns beep-beeping in free-form until the story found its way onto the deserted green lawns of the Alhambra to put its face into the ice-cool reflection of the Sierra Nevada Mountains in an ornamental lake.

The third story can wait.

The Holy Ground

ITS SURFACE BURNED his feet. He called it The Holy Ground.

Each glassy grain of sand was an oven fired by the sun and walking over it by day, his feet sank into its hot, slow surface. At night it was cooler but still as toilsome to walk across. Grass lumped and tufted in small dunes beneath conifers which encircled the central area as if keeping guard. There was always a stillness which made him want to talk aloud to whatever might be listening. He never met anyone else crossing The Holy Ground. There was something potent there that not so much inhabited The Holy Ground but was, actually, *it*. He found no menace in the place but had a notion that it *wanted* him. On getting through it he sometimes shook himself as if physically shrugging off something and on turning around would stare back at the sandy yellow drum expecting... well, he never knew. Times were that he skirted around the place but mostly he didn't think of The Holy Ground until he was on it, walking heavily, slower and sinking into its stomach.

Years earlier, as a boy and in a different country, his holy ground had been a grass field lined in white lime and crowned at each end with goal posts that had nets which sizzled when the ball broke into them: his favourite sound. Sometimes he would stay out longer when the rest of the team had gone to get changed, repeatedly making a net sizzle.

That was then.

Hot days clung together like wet plastic sheets and

were indistinguishable from each other as the summer season sweltered tourists in and out of the resort.

The holiday reps did their best, but cannon fodder they were. Sometimes he felt sorry as he witnessed them encircled by outraged holidaymakers, done out of some deal in the brochure. Such people operated on the age-old adage, *if you can't get to the heart of the problem, then tear the heart out of someone to do with the problem.* For some that was satisfaction enough. He was audience to this spectacle many times.

That day was extra hot. The heat had him. Vision cleared then blurred. He sat down but felt like a pendulum swinging out of control. The reps were being savagely gored – a cancelled bullfight. Some people just want blood.

He landed hard on the seat of his pants on hot dusty ground enclosed by ramshackle fences and wooden carts. Beyond were white walled buildings with terracotta tiled roofs that took the brunt of heat from an unconcerned sun.

People, lots of people, were shouting, whistling, hooting and waving straw hats from the other side of the barricades. Some had climbed the rooftops, balanced like bent aerials.

He scrambled quickly from the open ground through the spokes of a cartwheel and tumbled onto his belly to stare out. The Alamo this wasn't but he had dropped into some other event equally as climactic. He could now see the mustard-coloured ground was a village square that had been turned into a makeshift plaza de toros where crazed maletillas, wide eyed with hunger and bravado would hurl themselves into the capea season against hired bulls. He saw them, ragged and thin, brown-skinned and on fire with importance. Boys taking their first nervous steps on a holy ground that might, one day, take them to Madrid, not in the tatters they now wore, but in a Suit of Lights. Today this beggar's arena in this rat-scurried village was as good as Hollywood.

Men at one end of the plaza pushed a cart slowly away revealing the entrance to a yard. Another two men, heads out like terrapins, peeped into the yard.

The noise flattened.

There was silence followed by a shuffling sound.

Silence.

The gap to the yard waited then exploded into wide-horned blackness.

The bull tore into the plaza sending the maletillas scurrying over the barricades as the crowd sucked in continents of air. The beast's loaded shoulders thrust from its slim waist and muscled flanks sported a huge head spread with certain death, thrown up and down in rage – more than the young bullfighters had bargained for. It smashed the massive horns into the walls of the bullring, splintering the wood that had only seconds before formed a safe stockade. The crowd crackled to life, cheering wildly as the eyes of the young maletillas glazed with a different emotion. The bull circled the enclosure a few times, returning to the same spot each time. It had found its querencia. That it would defend. From there it would charge. The bull had found its holy ground.

From his place looking between the wheel spokes, he saw a man wave a handkerchief. Four of the twelve maletillas moved onto the hot arena. The other eight were already on their sad way back to the villages they had so gloriously left only days before.

The crowd howled with one contorted voice each time the creature tossed the first two young fighters and went wild as the bull sent the third high through the air into spectators on the shaded side, a swipe of blood splattering them.

The fourth maletilla, gangly and skinny, stood his ground.

The bull erupted into a charge.

Some people covered their eyes with hands as the beat of hooves drummed the afternoon. The slight body of the young boy was motionless.

Three feet away the bull dipped its head and angled its horns. The boy sprang up, summersaulted completely over the beast's back, landed safely on his feet, bowed extravagantly and stiffly and then walked out of the arena, leaving the bull tearing at thin air.

Not classical bullfighting, but brave and new!

The crowd boomed in applause.

His vision swam like ice murmured in whisky as he came to. He was still seated and sat a while longer allowing his faculties to gain command.

Over the way a rep he hadn't seen before swung his voice like a matador's cape dispatching each of his angry customers around his body with a wave of his arm.

Veronica!

Pase por alto!

Olé!

Crimson on White

DAYS WERE HOT and nights hardly cooler. Time was a molten sensation that trickled.

He sat in the shade of a bar slaking chilled beers, trying to minimise exertion. He had a good idea of what it was like to be oven-ready and cooking. What he looked at wobbled in the heat and lifted a little from the ground leaving a silver toenail of itself. Far off a tall house swayed like a cobra and telegraph poles made vision a snake pit. He took an extra deep gulp of his drink and read a few lines of his latest letter from home. They were always written on blue, onion skin airmail paper and felt so delicate.

The children grow day-by-day and love playing in the garden, though we're still in jumpers here...

Back home everything had an ordered time — seasons in which different sets of clothes were worn and days that organised themselves into neatly recognisable compartments: morning, afternoon, evening. He hauled himself up, tearing his thoughts away from home, tipping the table nearly over. The empty glass slid.

He made his way to the talcum edges of the tideless sea, its surface glinting lazily through a film of oil donated by hundreds of bathers. He shuffled on leaving behind coiled patterned footprints from his espadrilles. Beach colours were downbeat that year, nothing garish or loud, it was cut down, frayed denims, a take me as I am look, which he felt comfortable with.

She looked Swedish and blond and had taken the denim look to its extreme, her tanned skin covered in shreds. She walked towards, then past him releasing a smile that took the temperature even higher.

The apartment he rented was ground floor of a low-rise block stuck out on its own, at the end of a track, half a mile from town. The land either side of the track was rock and dust as if cleared for construction then left. Nothing much grew there other than brown spikes of grass. The isolation of the low-rise was a haven for the lonely. There were no children, three empty apartments, above him two ageing winos (she was young but you wouldn't know it) and next to his flat a woman in her twenties who sobbed for hours on end through each night, the paper thin walls doing little to suppress the sound. The sea cut a tiny horseshoe bay under his balcony which should have made sitting out there paradise but at night, on the surrounding rocky desolation, opaque bodies crawled, never upright and never moving but slowly. This was the block time forgot. One night, returning late, he entered his apartment only to catch a pale bent shape slip over the balcony. He bought chains and padlocks the next day.

*

The letters from home weren't delivered to the low-rise, he picked them up at the Rio Grande Bar in Calle San Antonio, a service supplied by its owner, Des. It had been friendly of Des to offer all that time ago and there seemed no need to change the arrangement. Des explained it was safer to have mail dropped off in town and anyway the postie was happy not to do the extra journey out of town and along the track. The other low-rise inhabitants had similar arrangements at the same bar.

'Espresso with a Drambuie on the side and mail touching down on runway one; full breakfast circling above and waiting.' Des had been reading an in-flight magazine left by a rep, 'Another hot one.'

'Yeah.'

He sat at the bar, stood the blue envelope against the Drambuie glass and stared at it as he drank his coffee. After drinking his coffee, he slid the glass from behind the envelope and swigged the sweet liqueur down in one, continuing to gaze at the blue rectangle which lay flat in front of him. He picked it up and slipped it into a book, taking the previous letter out, scrunching it up and tossing it on the floor.

'Two eggs, bacon, beans, tomatoes, fried bread waiting at terminal two.' The plate clattered down below a waxing grin from Des.

The day addled and clotted to evening. The evening dragged itself into night.

He woke up. Something was wrong.

He burst from the bedroom to the lounge: stillness. He rattled the chains and padlocks on the balcony doors. What was wrong? He listened at his front door, held his breath, and yanked it open: nothing. He closed the door and checked the padlocks and chains again.

Eventually he slept after listened hours, poised to every creak in the building. The heat was getting to him.

The next day burned his nostrils as he breathed it in. *The Great Artist* had painted the sky an unblemished blue, as if the words had fallen off his letters and the paper had been ironed flat onto the heavens. Nothing further off than fifteen feet held its form. The air melted.

He had a couple of stops before the Rio Grande to put the heat in check with shade and cold beers. At the second bar he was impaled by a female stare from a few tables away. She was dissolving, as women did on this island, down her neck and into the V of her handkerchief sized cotton top. It was his next-door neighbour at the low-rise. He smiled and she smiled back. As if flicked by a switch the heat turned sensually higher, but he was lazy and out of practice. *This is as good as it gets,* he thought, hoping she would make the first move. She didn't and the moment, beautiful as it was, passed. He watched her leave.

Des jumped, scattering blue writing paper behind the bar. 'I didn't expect you,' he said confrontationally.

Breakfast was ordered but took much longer than was usual as Des cleaned up soundtracked by the unmistakable sound of thin paper being crumpled. 'This is the hot one that starts the rest of the hot ones. From today we microwave.'

'No letter?'

'Today, er, no,' Des replied hesitantly as he put the coffee and Drambuie over the bar.

Breakfast was good as ever, but something was different: an itch not scratched.

He left The Rio Grande, surrendering himself to the heat and became lost in a slow walk and thoughts he would not be able to remember. The sun blistered the sky and the world wilted. This was 'the hot one', the day that might ignite a revolution or persuade a man he could fly from the top of a building.

...have to rush to the shops before they close.
He folded the paper rectangle, tucked it into its envelope and replaced it in his book.

Evening was hotter and slower than slow as he walked along the track. Ahead of him the sun was immense and about to drown itself in the sea. The low-rise looked like a severed foot.

Hot stagnant air blasted his face as he opened the apartment door, knocking him back a step. The chains and padlocks were almost too hot to handle as he struggled to release them. He flung everything and anything that would open, wide, and stepped out onto the balcony. The huge sun, almost purple, squatted on the horizon, swollen in its energy.

*

She wasn't crying, that's what was wrong!
Last night he hadn't figured it but tonight he put his finger right on it. Something had happened. Something was wrong. He moved quickly out of his apartment to

her front door, knocked and waited: knocked again and again. Took the handle; the door opened. The room was empty. He found and hit the light switch.

Every wall in the room, ceiling too, was covered in handwritten letters on blue onionskin paper, *his* letters, the discarded ones thrown on the floor of The Rio Grande. The place was a scrapbook of obsession.

He spent uncounted minutes of disbelief reading familiar lines before finding her note, written on heavy white paper.

We lived either side of each other's sadness. I wept for you.

There was no signature, only the pressed transfer of her lipstick-lips, crimson on white paper.

IOU

THE HILLS BEHIND FUENGIROLA swell like half-buried eggs scattered from a spilled basket and have lots of swimming pools. The swimming pools have detached houses beside them and shone cars in driveways. Gardens are manicured, sprinkled, and each has a strategically placed palm tree. The pools stare blinklessly upward to blue sky that stares back. There is little coming and going on the clean streets that service the houses and few residents are to be seen.

There is an atmosphere of unreal perfection.

A pueblo called Mijas sits prettily but higher in those hills. It was there long before the rash of pooled housing, its cramped dwellings compress against each other in jumbled neighbourliness on either side of its narrow streets and steep inclines.

Charles lives there. He appears to have the comfort of a private income, that is, he does no work but has money to spend – usually on other people. As such he often runs out of cash but always knows someone close at hand who can loan him.

Charles is a polite, gentle person whose conversation is easy and occasionally he can be heard to slip in that his family have racehorses on several hillsides further inland but that he has nothing to do with his parents any longer. Tall, with an unhealthy equatorial tan that never turns darker than liverish yellow and sleepy eyes like Peter Lorre, Charles has a system he works downhill on the coast between Fuengirola and Los Boliches.

He's a regular at about fifty bars and uses them as loan facilities, borrowing money from one, spending a little there then visiting other places where he owes, paying back debts in hard cash with the newly borrowed cash. Always, there's a free drink for him when he settles a bill.

This crossed bank accounting keeps him in the good life every night until the early hours of morning when single women hang their long, brown, tired legs from tall stools in the latest of late-night drinkeries. There is a tragic beauty, lack of pretence and hushed outpouring of humanity at these places in these final swept-up, closing minutes. It's witnessed in a customer's silent thought over a drink that is hard held and sipped only occasionally as the barman wipes down and cleans up. There is no better time to pick up a story, to feel its warm telling breathed closely over your face. Lonely is lonely and no question, but there's those that will yarn and there's those that like to listen. That last drink gets sweeter with the tincture of sadness. Charles had seen many such nights.

Because he brings customers with him, the bar owners like Charles and always see a profit for their investment in him. However, once in a while the system hiccups and a cash-strapped owner demands immediate repayment. At such times Charles whisperingly reminds the bar owner just *who* put money into the till by bringing in fast-spending customers. If that didn't work, Charles would rise to his full height and theatrically boom out, 'Damn you and all I've done for you!' dismiss the loan as peanut repayment, then stride out of the premises.

It never took him long to find a replacement venue.

Bankruptcy too would also come to his assistance, when, several times each year Shangri-La seeking Brits found the economic sour side of life on the Costa and would have to leave very quickly with only a small suitcase and a one-way ticket home. At such times, amid deserted dreams, curled slackly around the inside of a wine glass, on a shelf above weary bottles of spirits, would be an IOU signed, Charles.

Reader, have you been to such places? If so you have most likely been within spitting distance of Charles. He might even have bought you a drink.

Next time you are in a bar on that strip of southern Spain, between Fuengirola and Los Boliches, gaze up to the mirrored shelf behind the counter and look for a glass holding a furled slip of paper and win yourself some extra spending money; bet the barman, put on a meaningful stake, you can tell him whose name is signed on the IOU.

Take it Handy

THE JUG OF PUNCH was a small tunnel of a bar that served the world's best Irish Coffee.

Peter and Maggie were the salt and pepper owners of the enterprise and stood from mid-morning until the early hours of the next day trying to make matters pay.

'It's but standin' idle if there's no one to put a pint over,' Peter would say.

The Jug of Punch had small photographs of the home-country hung on the walls, a miniature Irish Harp on display above a row of Irish whiskeys and served green beer on St. Patrick's Day.

It would be great to say The Jug of Punch was a raucous watering hole for fired-up musicians, all-seeing poets, modern day philosophers and radical political thinkers, but it never was.

Not least, The Jug of Punch had been conceived with a hairline crack that leaked so very, very, extremely slowly – the loss not detectable in any way that would convince a person. But there it was in the long days, standing beside and between Maggie and Peter on nights when the bar was empty of custom for hours on end.

It was a creature of liquid darkness, a shadow thrown across water and of no definite shape. Sometimes the shadow tapped a slow upright dance from table to table as it moved about The Jug of Punch before shrinking itself into the landscape of one of the pictures on the wall. This was no fancy.

The late nights and early mornings were full of contemplation and too slowly drunk to make a profit. On those nights danced feet worked their way through the bar, the shapeless shadow projected on Peter's tired, closed eyelids.

One night a fat Irishman from Tarragona visited and captivated the few drinkers with tales of genius. He spoke of a single broken heart and the listeners found its shards within each of their chests. He told of a fantastic fish that had all but been caught but wriggled free at the very last second and asked his listeners if they knew of it? They did. Each one nodded. One or two even said they had *been* that fantastic fish. Everyone stayed late and drank well as they listed to story after story from the fat Irishman. Last and very late the best Irish Coffees in the world were served.

'Take it handy,' Peter's usual farewell to good custom, saw the fat Irishman gone whilst people were still talking about his final story.

The shadow had not danced that night.

From then on custom was better in The Jug of Punch and on St. Patrick's Day an orange VW camper parked outside, the driver spending a long thirsty evening drinking green beer served by Maggie and Peter. Maggie's face shone with the heavens in her eyes and the moon in her smile. The man from the camper saw a flock of orange and blue birds chasing a swarm of insects dance through Peter's eyes. He stared, waiting for someone else to notice but nobody did.

Two months later Peter and Maggie sold The Jug of Punch and returned to Ireland.

Four months after that the new owner of The Jug of Punch, unable to cope with spiralling debt and little or no custom, threw himself from an upstairs window to the street below. He died quickly.

People passing rushed to help. Others, unable to cope with the broken body, stood away. It was those people who saw a shadowy figure dance around the man, then away down the darkened street. But then, in the emotion of death, many things are said.

Caña = A Glass of Beer

SOMETIMES IT'S LANGUAGE that makes the world so big and distant, sometimes that is, when you're outside of its ordinary conversation and most revealing small talk. It's then you realise how foreign you are in the land in which you stand and at the mercy of not knowing a tiny noun, fumbling for a few letters to line up in your head to speed off the runway of your tongue and take flight.

Well, that was his experience...

The artist told him of perspectives and how time is best spent looking at a subject from as many angles as possible before deciding how it's going to be represented. Knowing he was an aspiring writer, she said, 'How a conversation of whispers becomes a screaming hurricane.' He was interested and that interest kept the two of them talking through the early afternoon as they sat under a parasol at a pavement café repeatedly ordering small dark cups of coffee and thimbles of Cointreau. She was teaching him, and he was her whole class.

'See what *your* eyes see and not what others would have you see on their behalf. Art by proxy is failed.' She raised her glass and gulped it dry. 'Your colours are a unique perception, only approximated by anyone else,' small flecks of saliva freckled his nose on each explosive p, 'so...' she wiped her mouth with the back of her hand, 'you assemble your palette for war and fire the colours in the cannon of the brush.' She hit the table sharply with her fingertips and jerked her head back in defiant gesture. She spoke of the many languages of the picture, the language of tone, line, contrast, pattern, as if they were the tongues of many different tribes that had come together to speak. She said, 'The artist, if clever enough, is able to use at least one and no more than three of the languages to bring the eyes nearer, the ears of the listener closer.' Her face ended up very close to his, challenging him to move back or come forward.

The situation dissolved into more talk and instruction, until she abruptly paid the bill, stood up and said, 'We go.'

She led him through hot streets of hush on that three o'clock Spanish afternoon.

At her apartment making love was restless. In the tideless minutes between renewed bouts of passion, in the rock pools of sheets, they gathered words like driftwood and made small fires of conversation.

The room was empty of clutter, only essentials of bed, two chairs and a small wooden table disturbed the landscape of white walls and bleached wooden floor. There were no paintings. 'The *memory* of all my work is here,' she said as if answering his unspoken question, 'my art now is with people.'

He thought for a few moments then said, 'Sometimes things aren't so complicated. What would you do with a glass of beer?'

She smiled knowingly at her new student, 'Drink it,' she replied.

They went down and out into streets yawning out of siesta, to the nearest bar.

She called out, 'Dos cañas por favor!'

They held the slippery glasses, chinked them together and emptied each in a gulp.

A Wedding at Al Gorrobo

ANNA HAS THE DARK SKIN of the desert night and wears a wedding dress from the winter peaks of the Sierra Nevada. Though old enough not to, she smiles to please, giggles, sits with her legs apart and today has the filigree of one hundred-year-old lace dangled from a headdress upon her cheeks, neck and shoulders. Her evening-brown hair is entwined with simple flowers.

Anna enjoys the feel of her almond-shaped fingernails which are stroked, each one, over its camber then along its manicured edge. At intervals they are drummed upon the table. Other times they chime the bell of a wine glass. The energy of her young being pulses on the side of her neck. Her thoughts track seconds, minutes and hours of this day that will alter many things.

She is Andalucian. She is pragmatic, but would not recognise the word, and knows the sour taste of poverty, the empty stomach of a missed opportunity.

She will marry.

So much is said to her by so many people. Trays of cold drinks are woven between tables. She wonders whether anyone will remain sober enough to remember the ceremony. Only her brother is representing her family. She stares at him as if insisting all details are forever retained for telling of how grand her wedding is. Anna wears her wedding like a suit of lights.

She thinks and her eyes fill with those thoughts of childhood and how she had run speedily in and out of its forest of torn moments and shredded ambitions. She recalls scavenging leftovers on plates from pavement cafés, running this way and that with her five-year-old hand cupped to every foreigner, eager for the smallest of coins and when a little older longing for the day when she would have full hips and breasts like the female tourists. How they swung their handbags with such little compassion. Anna thinks and her eyes moisten with those thoughts.

The lawns of the tennis club hiss with conversation, like they do on other days with sprinkled water, as people dressed in strong colours are clutched around tables spread with white cotton and centred with flowers of deep indigo and gold petals. This is how it is on a wedding day.

On *this* wedding day.

Anna sits, crystal, in a chair of her choosing and has abandoned much of what she is and knows little of what lies ahead, but she has had to gamble many times in her life. Today she will marry a foreigner and is clueless of how he earns his money, how he earns *so much money*, or why he should fall in love with her — but then, love gives no reasons.

Her soon-to-be husband, even today, is talking in harsh whispers to his men friends. They are often to be found like this but always turn round with white smiling mouths when interrupted.

However, Anna has *seen things* and has stored those memories in many hiding places where they will remain, always available, an investment should they be required.

She has set these matters aside for an emergency.

DJ Hiatus

THE SILENCE BETWEEN RECORDS hung like a storm about to show its power.

The tight knot of heads fighting to be heard at each table in El Climax eased back in comfortable conversation without battling against the music. It was another world in there behind the heavy wooden door with its gangster flap peephole. Dark morning lapped sluggishly outside but inside, night's losing war against daylight was kept alive under a ceiling of low glows.

El Climax was where he came in the small hours of morning after doing his long sets, singing and playing guitar to holiday makers in the bustling resort. It was a gay bar but used by local Spanish staff of whatever persuasion as an after-hours watering hole to meet, relax and spend their tips. He always felt good there amongst the all-Spanish clientele and enjoyed their after-work enthusiasm. It was impossible to keep up with their chit chat but then she, his chief reason for going there, spoke to him in English.

The season was drawing to an end, and she had things to say, things that were hard to say but things that *had* to be said. She dropped her gaze to the table then up to meet his, 'Always?'

'Yes, with you,' he replied.

'No end to the season? No end?'

He shook his head, smiled then kissed her reassuringly.

'And when winter barks? Wineless nights and cheap meals? Summer colours run from washed out clothes in the sink of an apartment coldly rinsed in thin rays of a wasted sun?' She continued, 'Money argued over when I buy a lipstick? Do you know that time? That time cleaves the year and frosts passion like a marriage. At that time fruit has long-left summer's heavy branch and sniping winds rifle down from the mountains to rattle empty streets of wet concrete and cotton jackets are cold on your back. You will hear that wind moan its lonely tale in your gold-ringed ear and begin to find your own words to leave.'

'Never!' he said urgently, shocked by what he was hearing.

'And when Spanish smiles are zipped, saved for the start of the next season, and eyes stare along the wet promenade, heartbroken over summer, what will make you happy?'

'You! *You* will make me happy,' he replied despairingly.

She took his hand, placed it on her breast saying, 'Yours, and these lips,' she kissed him, 'my hips curved for your dance. You are so powerful now, with your songs that fill the bars each night with happy people. But when winter arrives you will be ordinary. There will be no tourists to crow over you. I will speak in my language with my friends, our words will crack like whips before laughter, leaving you in the ugly shadow of ignorance and you will be unable to warm yourself on our fiery breath.' She paused, 'Estranjero.'

Her last word was cold.

He knew that word.
Knew it meant *foreigner*.

At that moment a record broke through:

Gonna take a little time / Time to think things over…

The DJ had got his act together.

Only a Tale

TELLING TALES IS ONE THING but who they are told to is another.

Beyond everyday mischief and the, 'Don't say I told you...' prefix of good gossip that inevitably would find its way out, regardless, is information guarded by the unofficial secrets act.

Where the line begins or ends and how far it can be pushed before it breaks is anybody's guess. The consequences too are unknown forces, easily agitated combustible atoms capable of utmost wasting and those that do get wasted are often the lucky ones. Survivors live on, charred with misgivings, and blistered by memories.

He had seen the name on his map and liked the sound of it so he headed there.

The once small, sleepy village of Arroyo de la Miel, translated means *stream of honey*, had lost its sweetness in a rage of land and property deals that flung it into the twentieth century.

New streets of unfinished pavements and dodgy road surfaces criss-crossed each other in brutal straightness with not a curve in sight, fast traffic replacing yesterday's donkey-slowness. The bodies of dogs and cats were pulped and flattened forever into highway history. Sometimes a huge dust-belching lorry only caught the back half of an animal, the creature's hell-death squeezed through its mouth in a choked, horrific last scream.

Graceless, multi-storied buildings dominated the ever-shrinking sprinkle of traditional houses, small and threatened by the cuckoos of concrete.

Workers snowed by cement dust were animated statues, lifting, carrying, shovelling, trowelling like ants in concert, their thick sweated hair dripped on muscled necks mapping them in rivulets. Most were migrant workers from Andalucia, paid in regular cash and cheap apartments in which they crammed their families who argued to pass their imprisoned time. Wives once married to straight-backed horsemen now set meals for spavined and saddle-backed husbands.

This was a place where crane, JCB and dumper were dictators amidst tornadoes of dust swirled up by machinery and traffic relentlessly forcing dysfunctional property upwards. Decay gnawed away before completion. Windows jammed half closed and flushed toilets rose to a shriek away from overspill, then subsided to a muddy pool of sewage.

Progress! The mayor of Arroyo de la Miel had seized upon the word — *change* would have been more appropriate. He had only just over a year to fatten himself from his office before possible deselection in the municipal elections. *Progress!*

Behemoth fortresses went up faster and faster.

Interestingly, a minor official had gone public, stating that the *revolutionary progress initiative* in Arroyo was out of control. He and his family left town 'quietly' and were not heard of again. Close relatives living nearby suddenly became proud owners of the latest model Seat cars had to offer and made no fuss regarding the whereabouts of their kin.

Winter came colder than usual as the weakened sun hardly penetrated mushrooming clouds of finely pulverized construction matter. Children shivered days away and slept foetal through nights, hugging warmth closely to their bone-chilled bodies. Some old people gave up.

Three months prior to the elections the mayor stopped all construction, declared a holiday, issued a warm clothing allowance and also a heating allowance to all families in town.

He secured the Easter election, retaining his office.

*

Daydreaming in his VW camper whilst on his journey away from Arroyo de la Miel, the traveller imagined it in future years when cafés bloomed on the safe-paved streets of restricted traffic, their tables seated with families enjoying happy times; fountains of sun-sparkled water spouting the town's clean air as children ran in and out to cool themselves. Elsewhere gardens and parks luxuriantly green and splashed purple or magenta by bougainvillea and scented by bergamot would be walked by lovers. He even daydreamed there was a big shining statue of the mayor.

But this was only a daydream, and the story of Arroyo de la Miel is only a tale.

August Fishermen

ESCAPE IS A SLEEPY Mediterranean village set in dusty tiredness where time hangs unsettled and where a letter lies open to be re-read on a table.

One bus out and one bus back each day. Always someone checks who gets off.

The only bustle is the return of a fishing boat, its hull scraping up the beach to release baskets to the white smiles of children, eyes wide with excitement and voices shrill with praise. This is a place where a fisherman commands respect. He is the agent whose dawn exit goes unnoticed but whose return is that of a great warrior. Soon the village women will surround a makeshift stall calculating the meals that can be made from the least spent money. The younger women are more carefree – their time will come.

The fishermen wash down, coil ropes and make good the small boat for tomorrow, then go to the seafront café to drink strong black coffee and smoke pungent cigarettes. They play dominoes and cards and talk to the older men, fathers, grandfathers, uncles, exchanging knowledge and stories about fish. There are loud exclamations but no arguments. There is no laughter – that will arrive later after sleep, fresh clothes, and wine.

Meanwhile a single tourist picks up the letter from the table in front of him and lets its message drape his mind. He looks over the blue onion skin paper to the spangled blue sea thinking deeply between the two.

The air murmurs.
Sounds are slow.
There is forever here.

Finding the Lost World

THE BOY WAS FULL of dinosaurs.

It was a wrestle to hear him get his tongue around the names, though his mind had been entwined by them for quite some time. Those young eyes alive with it, like it was now and the chance of seeing one of those lumbering leviathans, good.

He was infectious and brought out the boy in Harry, that whole romance, the possibility of everything and anything in the blink of a moment.

The boy's mother and father loved him. Loved to hear him talk with such enthusiasm; saw how he lit up other people as he spoke to them; saw how other people strolled almost forgotten roads of childhood as the youngster began his routine. This is what the boy could do.

Harry had been audience to the kid but was now talking to the father.

'So you like walking,' Harry said.

'Don't get the time to do much of it these days. Y'know after work I'm only good for a stiff drink and a comfortable chair in front of the telly,' replied the father.

'Yeah?'

Harry did a couple of miles each day and felt smug about it. The idea of walking out along the lane from the holiday apartments, to strike up to the hills a few miles off was as good a way as any to get to know the young guy.

It was not long before the two of them were out to

where the surfaced road stopped, and the track began and didn't stop until the top of the hill.

The father was younger than Harry and, though Harry didn't push it, the father did well considering the guy didn't do this sort of thing regularly. In fact the young man didn't break into heavy breathing anywhere along the way. Even if he had Harry wouldn't have heard him over his own laboured breath.

'I start chuffing pretty quickly,' said Harry, 'then go into this breath-beat that my mind sings, "Don't Stand So Close To Me". Y'know, The Police tune?'

The father chuckled and they kept moving, stamping short, sure steps into the inclined dirt.

Rain, the day before, had been torrential causing fast run-off that had cut ruts into the track and heaved up stones and rocks. Elsewhere fans of washed debris decorated the ground.

Harry wanted to say, 'Must have been terrific to walk in as the water flowed downhill,' but didn't. Why would anyone say that? It was hard enough to climb a hill as steep without added problems of water rushing against you. But in his mind the picture was formed. That's the way he had it, he tilting against the landscape and the weather.

Harry was breathing hard by the time they got to within a hundred metres from the top, but not a sound from the young father, other than the regular swish, swish of his sports shorts.

They cut across some open ground that looked a better bet than the track which dipped a little then rose sharply to the crest of the hill.

Arriving at the top was good. The views out in all

directions magnificently soaked up and a few photographs taken, as if the two were Edmund Hillary and Tenzing Norgay. They didn't say much, only punched the air, high-fived, that sort of thing.

Absurdly, perhaps due to exhilaration, Harry remembered an old girlfriend from his single days, before Sally. Rosalyn... She was wild, but then so was he.

'*Yeah, gotta know. Yeah, gotta know. Rosalyn.*' The whole song by The Pretty Things became a performance in his mind, maraca-shaking his hands, his sixty-two-year-old hips snaking to pulse. Wow! Rosalyn! He'd forgotten this...how it felt.

Discovery is nothing but its own trip. Harry was out there. This was not nostalgia; it was an erupting hormone hit.

On the way down Harry said, 'You did well. You must be pretty fit.'

'Well, I nearly got to singing that Police tune,' said the young father.

That was good of him. Harry thought then of the father and the son and the capacity both had for this, to make you feel young.

They arrived back at the apartments. Harry showered and the young father engaged his wife and son in some of the happenings on the walk.

Much later that evening, after a meal on the veranda and as Harry and Sally were clearing up, the whole family came by. The boy got straight into his rap on dinosaurs and everyone's eyes caught fire.

Darkness settled around them. Harry found his equilibrium once more and felt a little meek. He stared at the boy, then at the father, wondering about relationships and the inevitable cracks. Harry looked at his wife, silently puzzling whether she had a male equivalent of 'Rosalyn'.

At that moment Sally turned to him, face-on, and gave Harry an inexplicable smile.

Starting with a Fine Hat

HE SEATED THE HANDSOME, broad-brimmed, straw hat firmly on his head and sat next to the rail looking over it as the boat moved out of Skiathos.

All day before, a wind had bumped itself over the island and the sea was still in response. Soon spray from the bow spattered over passengers. They shrieked with pleasure, young girls laughing white-teethed mouths into the welcome faces of boyfriends.

The man with the fine straw hat held it firmly on his head, knowing if he didn't it would be whisked into the air then bounced across the Aegean.

The pitching boat began to yaw at about an hour out as it made a route between Skopelos and another island. The sea mixed there, and troughs deepened. Quite a few poor sailors had gone down with sickness and, as if a plague had boarded, more took on that look that knows something's wrong inside — a kind of cut off from the world expression. You know when you see a person with that look, they are at a crossroads of discovery concerning mind and body. The former demands obedience of the latter. Do as I say! Those silent synapse-leapt signals swept aside by organs in revolt.

The man with the hat had changed hands several times and pressed his splendid Loro Piana Panama firmer onto his head, pulling it down at the back and now using his fingers like paper clips, holding the wind-curled brim at the front.

From out of sight, the female guide kept plugging

information and snippets of Greek mythology over the Tannoy... 'Aegeus threw himself into sea which now bears his name, on sighting the black-sailed vessel carrying home his triumphant son, Theseus, after slaying the Cretan Minotaur.' Apparently, it was a bungle of mixed messages and wrong coloured sailcloth. What would be the name of the Aegean Sea had that tragic chain of events not occurred?

As that ghost of a question faded, another, more contemporary tale squeezed through the sound system. 'Alonissos, over to the right, woke up to the twentieth century in 1971 when its first private car arrived: the first motor vehicle on the island. That landmark day was conjoined by a second similar day a few weeks later when a second car arrived. The potential for a traffic jam became *parle nouveaux* and a hip vocabulary of motor jargon soon began to work its way through the tavernas.

Sadly, fantastically, the Alonissos motor dream was shattered when the two brand new cars collided head-on after only a few days. The island reverted to donkey power.'

This guide was good. Those fit enough, chuckled.

Ideas of what the guide might look like invaded the passage.

It was about then that the boat began to behave very badly. Waves hit her broadside several times like telling body blows, the sort boxers put in, knowing that if the bout goes beyond the halfway mark, no matter how willing the spirit, an opponent's fists will hang punchless at the end of jelly-arms.

A lot more people were sick now and those that weren't *wanted* that distraction.

A new passenger had crept on board: fear.

Swinging north-west towards Skopelos Town, around a smashed promontory, new water from nowhere had the bows nose deep in it. The rear end bucked up into fresh air, courtesy of a trough that dropped away a sudden twenty feet. Gone.

The props raced in freedom: released lions.

GGRRRRRRRRRRRRRRRRRRRRRRRRRRRRRRRRRRRRRRRR

The boat spun on its nose like a whisky stick. Tables and chairs in the below deck lounge lifted. People levitated. Drinks hovered, gelled over cups and glasses, reminiscent of in-capsule film of space shots. Everything hung crazily in the air for one long, long, lifetime second before being sucked away.

WHAM! The spell broke.

Bodies, furniture, the whole lot were dumped into a pile of arms, legs and screams.

SLAM! The stern whacked down into water, propellers digging into sea again lifted the bows out of dive. The boat was back in business, however shakily.

Crew and others plunged in to sort out the debris of passengers and furniture. Crying, shaking and shock held many people for a long time.

Cuts bled.

Swellings rose.

Bruises blackened.

Crewmen fussed around handing out bottled water, making consoling hand gestures, speaking loudly, filling the place with authority whilst reassembling tables and chairs.

That was it.

As fast as it happened it was over.

There were no serious injuries.

Most talked it over and over, over once more, hardly listening to anything but their own words. They exorcised the demon of that moment, putting its twisted body away from their own.

The sea now ran with the boat chasing her to Skopelos harbour where the vessel signed in without the slightest quayside bump.

Off the gangplank people headed for welcome seafront tavernas to nurse themselves with alcohol and strong coffee, still talking about the event but now listening to each other.

The guide? She must have been in there somewhere.

This near disaster would never be leaked over the Tannoy.

The man miraculously still had possession of his hat, though now carried by hand, it wasn't so fine, but he held it carefully – some might say, gently.

The man and his hat had been through something, and he had a newfound relationship with it.

He would wear that hat and that hat wear him for many years to come.

Post

SHE PLACED THE SIX postcards, piled one upon the other picture-down, in a stack next to the biro.

'I never know what to write.'

Mary picked up the pen, rested her hand over the top postcard, the ballpoint a centimetre above the small writing space and cocked her head as if searching for something. It stayed like that for a few minutes.

'It's no good, I'm just not in the mood for this,' she said and looked out over the cactus beds to where a hummingbird hawk moth mined every Baltic-blue bloom of a plumbago shrub. It worked from flower to flower, its body a sculpture of stillness; wings a blizzard of movement. The moth refuelled in flight, burning its reserves so rapidly as it did so, the next stop vital to keep it airborne. So it became a slave to the plumbago plant.

The beds around the balcony were a geometry of leaves, mostly fleshy and spiked. Huge cacti poked skyward above the rest, supported by cord to the uprights of the balcony. There was every angle on display, acute, obtuse, reflex, and one plant even threw out limbs to elbows from which forearms made right angles, as if willing biceps to swell.

'I'll post those,' Terry said, bracing himself into the hot-air day, 'when I go for my walk.'

He walked every whatever-weather morning, his chance to think and straighten life out a little.

'I dreamed again,' Terry spoke.

'Tell me,' she said.

'It was on a canal narrow boat, the whole family, but I can only remember me, essentially, and we were with the McPhalls.'

'We haven't seen them in sixteen years!'

'But we were with them like it was today. Anyway, from the narrow boat we went to their flat and it was his birthday, cards all over the place hung like washing on lines of string across the room. I noticed one was from Vic Malcolm, who I don't know, but there was his name signed big on a card.'

'Vic Malcolm you say?'

'It was a long room, three feet-high windows the length of it either side, and a single long settee, very sparse but good and airy. I liked it. He looked as young as I remembered him, perhaps younger, and wearing a smart, grey, casual suit – grey with splashes of blue woven into the cloth. Stylish, Italian perhaps. He was about to leave to play his guitar and sing, his job, it was a solid situation that paid too. Then, without a flicker of hesitation informed me he had an electricity bill he could never pay off!'

'That sounds just like him,' Mary nodded. 'You didn't pay the bill for him, did you? You were always sorting his mess.'

'Well if I did it's only a dream, but no, I didn't,' Terry defended himself. 'Then, as he was telling me about the electricity bill, he slid down the back of the sofa, like he was paper-thin, but came up as quickly, only he had become a sort of ugly glove-puppet, large head, short body and gaping mouth. That was it.'

'Wonder where the McPhalls are?' Mary said, 'It all

ended so carelessly with them ...such a lot unsaid... real things unattended.'

'Comes down to survival,' Terry said, brushing Mary's reverie aside. 'The next dream had me at Tynemouth, at the end of Front Street, where it turns left and away from the priory.'

'You had another dream?'

'I told you, I dreamed. Anyway, where was I? Oh yes, it was a black & white dream, no colours, only tones between black & white, which I guess doesn't make it strictly black & white, but you know what I mean.'

Mary looked up, gazed into the distance, her eyes unfocused. *She* had dreams and one day she would tell Terry *her* dreams but today was not a day for that.

'So, there it is, end of Front Street, Tynemouth, in black and white, except it's China Town, busy as hell. Swarms of Chinese selling squawking, wriggling things live and cooking in open pots, serving hot food in small bowls. Smoke, noise, smells...busy, busy, busy. A bit like the stock market, hectic, and making money.'

Mary picked up a cold G&T, sweating in its tumbler, sipped it, replaced it on the damp coaster.

'Then, in all this confusion, I met Ollie. Big, broad-shouldered, confident Ollie – and Jim Naylor!'

Mary made wide eyes.

'I know, haven't seen him in 30 years! He was half hiding, crouched down, as if somebody was after him. He was in some sort of trouble. He was scared.' Terry frowned as if trying to recall a particular and important detail.

'The next thing is I'm involved in an escape from

China Town. Ollie was smoothing things over with locals as Jim & I squeezed and struggled through a seaweed of bodies. It got busier and busier, people closing in on us, getting darker till there was very little white... Then total blackness.'

Mary said nothing, but picked up her drink and took another sip. She looked away again into the distance without answering.

'I'll post those cards when they're ready,' Terry called back shutting the door behind him as he headed out for his walk.

'Fish

THE NET HOUSE STINKS of sea and weed from last winter's storms.

Not just this, the net house stinks of diesel, paint and machinery oil. The nose is a crude detector and is misled by the strongest overtones, not signal to the subtlety of things that seek to be concealed.

The last few of these wooden structures stand tall and haunt the east end of the harbour. Creosoted black, they are dark rockets, perhaps landing or at any moment, taking off.

Danny loves them.

Most of all he loves his.

He had been born within fifty metres of the highest, high tide mark in the year of his arrival and with that, and his family being fishermen for generations, had the right to a net loft and to make a living from it.

The sea holds no respect and shows it yet again in another Stamp Day.

Danny will visit the DHSS to argue a case of how he really wants to work but Poseidon has shut the factory gates.

His chance of getting a stamp is slim.

The man there, cloned from a lineage of civil servants, has some tap into a greater understanding of the local sea conditions, more so than the local fishermen.

Anyway, Danny reports, has his say. The man in the suit has his say. Neither listens to the other. Danny knows The Suit only stays confident, implacable, because of the double-plate glass separating them.

Who's captive in this zoo?

Back at the harbour waves excavate shingle and slew it high on the beach, against the harbour arm to the music of bumping bass beats of incoming breakers, followed quickly by brushed ride cymbals of waterspatter and the rolled-snare of back-drawn pebbles. A fleet of JCBs couldn't have done a better job.

The Boys Ashore who never go out to fish have gone to pubs or other jobs or both. They put themselves about, 'Any job a tenner'. They stack, carry, fill and load.

The fishermen are concerned about the day's loss and make small groups in and around the doorways of their huts, grumbling and arguing as they sip from grimy mugs of hot tea.

Eventually silences invade their brooding and they disperse.

The harbour seems to have become almost functionless to Danny.

He looks at the Heritage Sea Museum and mutters thanks that no children queue from its doors today, then gazes across to the Hello Sailor bar with its shone brass turnings and fastidiously neat-written blackboard menu, finally resting his eyes on Oysters Night Club which at this time of day is a coffin.

His disapproval of these places catering for an upwardly mobile clientele arriving like cuckoos to the harbour comes only second to his detestation of The Sea

Life Centre. *Tank 22: Bottom Feeders*, contains two gigantic monk fish that would, alone, pay for today's losses.

He looks around his harbour, speaks in an undertone, 'What's the council up to? This place is a freak show…a bloody circus.'

The whelk stall alone stands monument to the harbour's purpose. That so, Danny noticed last summer, Harold, who mans the stand, had taken to wearing a white glengarry, the sort they sport in McDonald's.

A few hours later the tide is pulled back and leaves boats with their sterns hanging naked from a cliff of newly sculpted beach. They need a bulldozer out to put some shingle back under before the next tide takes the boats away for rock bait.

A bad day all round for the industry. No local fish. Prices up at wet-fish shops and restaurants, as long distance huss, dab and sole are moved in by road.

Night gathers itself. The rope lights and neon ignite. The carnival is switched on. The money begins to arrive in BMWs and Range Rovers, turning the lumped and scarred harbour tarmac into an executive car park.

Danny smells the sea, smiles, 'If Chanel could bottle this…'

He has changed clothes and is unrecognizable as a fisherman. His Armani, Prince of Wales Check suit is perfect.

Danny slides the padlock off the net loft door, releasing the imprisoned essence of the harbour from inside. It comes out in a gasp. Not even Lassie could detect the cache. He picks up a small Tupperware sandwich box nested with cotton wool and containing five phials. 'Let's go for the big fish,' he mutters to himself.

Danny drives towards the motor launches in the marina, thirty miles down the coast where everything is designer and what's in his phials will more than cover the day's losses.

The Blues

THE FIRST FOUR BARS dangled him over the edge of existence.

Broken glass, razor swarf, steel needles, harpoons, hooks screaming for flesh, the bottleneck exploded over amplified strings, urgent as a new-born's first breath and anguished as a painful death. That contact between slide and string like the Everest of sex. There is nothing else.

Lenny played the blues because he knew how.

'The blues is a high water table never needing but a scratch to reach,' he would say. 'When you strike, it springs up without control. Before long you've let loose a stream which becomes a river which snuggles into a lake which gets so big it becomes an ocean. You try to mop it up in a song but you only make another ocean as you squeeze it out. Once you've found the blues it's yours till you die.'

His audience mumbled in agreement, 'That's right… a consumption…hell hound sniffing your trail…'

The Mojo Club had been home to Lenny every Tuesday night for the past three years during which time he had built a good following and now had the credentials of a white who *could* sing the blues. Tuesdays were prime for the blues. Money was short but the club's credit was good for its regulars and besides Tuesday was that pocket in the week when tension at work and relationships between couples seemed to come together in an outpouring of angst.

There were very few fights but plenty of couples slagging each other off – doing the dozens. The upshot of these spats, and Lenny never knew why it was always this way, was that the woman upped and left.

Now the man had the blues and the blues is a thirsty friend. The man would get drunk. He would get so stumbling drunk that it was Lenny's job to both see the guy home safely and to authenticate a slightly overworked tab, should one be running. Having steered the drunk home and up to his pit, Lenny often found the woman partner charged with gratitude, and what might begin with her saying, 'Would you like a drink?' would end in Lenny really popping his cork.

He began to have his regulars, his 'alley cats', and at one point things were so good he asked for a Monday night at the Mojo as well as his Tuesday spot, so that he could keep his customers satisfied.

The manager, turning down the request, shook his head, raised a stiff little finger in front of Lenny's face then curled it slowly down in limp fashion. Lenny was hip to what was unsaid.

Lenny sometimes toyed with his alley cats during the late, late hours of his performance, singing, 'Squeeze my lemons baby, till the juice runs down your legs' or other such classic blues lines. These cues along with the right look or nod would prompt a squabble, securing Lenny with his action for the small hours of the morning.

On one Tuesday, much the same as any other, Lenny was heavily into a self-composition, 'You're Looking at your Man', growling it out to one of his cats but must have swept a look and rocked a nod on the wrong word too many times at too many different cats.

Within minutes the Mojo sparked with gender flak. Faces were slapped, drinks poured over heads, chairs tipped over, followed by a rapid female evacuation. The night ground on to a tired end. The men left behind formed a scrum to support their insecure egos and paid no real attention to the blues.

Lenny made a decision not to go a-calling on any one lady friend that night for fear of offending another and heck, he couldn't visit them all!

Next Tuesday started slowly. Nine o'clock and only two strangers in the club. By ten they had drunk-up and gone. 'Let's go and look for some life,' the manager heard one guy say to the other. The club was empty. So it was through to midnight and beyond. The Mojo really did have the blues and closed early. The next week the same.

Where were they?

Lenny called a few regulars but only got answerphone replies.

By the third week Lenny was ready for the chop and got it.

'Perhaps you need a change Lenny,' whined the boss, 'come back in a few months eh? In the meantime I'm gonna try a country & western guy on Tuesdays. He's good, been packin them in at Jimmy's place down the river.'

Some departure from the blues, Lenny thought.

Two months later Lenny paid a courtesy call to the Mojo. He had plenty of work and to show there was no bad feeling he wanted to pay for a few rounds of drink and get up to do a request, if he was asked. He didn't get asked and didn't stay long.

The tall blond country & western singer was too good to shift and the audience back to capacity though perhaps fewer couples and more single women. Lenny saw a few of his ex-alley cats but they didn't notice him. No, their eyes were fixed on Chet 'Midnight Cowboy' Ray.

'The cowboy sure keeps the customers satisfied,' said the boss smugly as Lenny turned towards the exit.

An old bunkhouse blues filled Lenny's head: *Rocks is my pillows, Stones is my bed…*

Last Fair Deal Gone Down

SES THE CORPSE, 'Hey Robert, I got black, bootblack, soil under my back and night-black sky above like you. But you got blood about your body.'

Ses Johnson, 'Stay outa my ears crossroad creature. I'm movin on... just 'cidin which way to go.'

Ses the scrape-voice creature, 'Which ever you choose, you in a walkin blues, rambling on your mind, travelling riverside blues from four until late, wishin for a kind hearted woman... An all the time your love in vain.'

Ses Robert Johnson, 'Shake my shoes of you! Stamp the ground on you! Fill your mouth with stone! Make you hush in your quick-buried scrape! You in the crossroad of no escape!'

Robert Johnson falls upon his knees, hands clenched in prayer learned over hard years, feeling tides pounding in his ears, moaning words through long unlit hours, looking this way, then that way, then looking high above into the cold starry sky.

Robert Johnson has winter mud cracked over his young hands making them old; making fingers hard to bend. He knows there is no future with fingers that can't make quick whispers over his 50 cent guitar neck. Robert Johnson prays and bays like a hound fearing Hell. And all the time, between every break in his words the creature croaks in his ear, tempting him, doing the blues, taunting him. Another corpse, then another joins in.

Yells Johnson, 'Hell on your souls! You in the unhallowed ground of men that done no good, an' have no good word on your wormy tongues. Jump Jacks snappin your backs awake from the earth to spit an' talk dirt! Murderers every one!'

Robert Johnson remains at the crossroad, tortured by the eloquent tongue of the Devil as he speaks through the gone mouths of the trashed dead. Robert Johnson also hears something in the Devil's voice he recognizes. It is the shadow of his own voice. The womanizing voice he uses after playing-hours which fuels the music he plays in the juke joints.

He knows many women and has loved many women. He says it's not his fault, it's his condition. You pick up a guitar: you pick up a woman. It's a deal done.

It's in his voice calling:

A woman is like a dresser
Some men always running thro
Its drawers

'Now look here Robert, I can make rocks your pillows from now till forever. I can rain frogs and swamp on you thro' the night. I can flay your back with memories of Abbay & Leatherman plantation or, or…put honey of first love in your ear,' croons the Devil.

'This crossroads is no good place. Got a bad deal feel as good as X is a sign of a man's name against a paper to sell his life away. To sell his wife away!

To want her back to sell her again like a song traded in bar after bar for cheap liquor-coins. Who knows where this ends?'

The cold black night pours itself around Johnson's shivering body, creaking trees and snaking through the hobo-brush jungle, shaking the stars out of the heavens to frost moon-shone rail lines that lead all the way to the rich north.

'You see your way?' ses the Devil's Dead. 'You see your way to Canada to troubadour a land clean of The Klan, where cotton dust don't sit in your lungs an' where a noose ain't hung lazy over the branch of a bull bay tree.

You put your sign like Jesus upon all time an stop your hangin round this crossroads. A small cross is all's needed to nail you to eternity.

Try signin in the air.

Try signin in the earth.

Try signin on your heart.'

'OK, OK, but what deal's a-goin down?' ses Robert Johnson 'I ain't got little above n below the soul of my shoes.'

'Soul,' ses the Devil. 'Sooooooooul.' Licking his lipless lips with his tongueless tongue, the Devil thinks thinkless things, 'You have y'self Robert an you can give y'self to any heart you want. Don't be out of heart, you can lose your heart to a good-heart, a sweetheart. Give your heart from the bottom of your heart, wear it on your sleeve, take heart don't eat your heart out over some heart-breaker!

This here's a heart to heart talk Robert.

Learn my words by heart an' set your heart on what I say instead of standin there chicken all over with your heart in your boots. You a man after my own heart an enjoy women an' song. I'll throw both in. Do it with heart an' soul. Sayin this once an no more Robert, from the heart of *my* heart.'

Whether Robert Johnson gives his consent to the proposition or if he is sweet-talked into sleep, his head nodding in agreement as his eyes close, nobody knows but the Devil seizes the moment.

The dark-heart deal is done.

Next morning Robert Johnson wakes with a dew blanket over him and sweat on his face.

He is alone except for the perfectly curved body and long slim neck of a Sears & Roebuck Stella guitar lying next to him and an **X** scored deeply into the earth of the crossroad.

In November 1936, in a San Antonio hotel, Robert Johnson records twenty-nine tracks with Don Law for Vocation Records. He works regularly, dresses well, is popular, drinks and enjoys the company of women.

He is poisoned in Greenwood, Mississippi August 16th 1938.

Testament. All who hear him say the Devil plays his deal through Robert Johnson, jerking and plucking each finger on each noted string and wailing torturously in vocals

Got to keep movin
Got to keep movin
Blues fallin down like hail

Got to keep movin
Got to keep movin
Hellhound on my trail

*

It is Wednesday 25th July 1965 in the men's toilet of The Pontiac Club, Zeeta House, Putney. A fourteen-year-old kid from Newcastle recognizes the guy zipping up at the urinal. Without hang up he flips out a flimsy diary and asks for an autograph. The two chat about blues and especially blues singer Robert Johnson before going into the club's live music lounge. The kid shuffles near the small stage along with a few other punters whilst the guy from the toilet tunes his Sunburst Gibson Les Paul. What happens during the next 45 minutes defies description. The guy plays guitar like nobody has ever played guitar. The small audience is rock-still in awe.

Near the end of the set the guy steps up to a mic, nods to the kid, mumbles, 'I'm at the crossroad,' sings Robert Johnson's 'Ramblin On My Mind'.

The guitarist leaves the Bluesbreakers four days later. John Mayall plays the Pontiac Club the following week with a new guitarist.

Standing at the crossroad the guitarist makes a new deal. He will summon a magic to make a 'Strange Brew' of music for the years ahead.

The baton of The Devil's Music, passed to Robert Johnson, is palmed to new keeping.

It is Sunday, 31st July 1966 at The Royal Windsor Racecourse, Windsor, Berkshire. Ten thousand people have turned up for the 6th National Jazz & Blues Festival. The fourteen-year-old kid from Newcastle is now fifteen and stands in that audience. The early evening sky remains clear, as thunder explodes from the crowd, heralding the debut performance of a three-piece group. The guitarist wears white bell-bottom trousers and a flash, silver jacket, spawned from his new deal. He plugs a Gibson Les Paul into a Marshall stack, carves the opening riff of 'Spoonful' into the air, and whips up slavish worship from his devotees.

The fifteen-year-old from Newcastle gathers a lungful of air, 'Play Robert Johnson!' he bawls through the drowning bedlam of appreciation.

By a magic darker than Black Mass from a Black Jack Scrub oak thicket, the words take flight on raven wings through the din.

'This one's for anybody who likes Robert Johnson.'

'From Four Until Late' rumbles and darkens the atmosphere.

It is 2004. The guitarist records 14 of Robert Johnson's songs. The CD from those recordings are issued on the Reprise label under the title, *ME AND MR JOHNSON*. The cover artwork is by Peter Blake and shows the guitarist, shirt, tie and suited, guitar on lap, sitting in similar pose to a portrait of Robert Johnson which is hanging on a wall behind. The guitarist is fifty-nine years of age. The portrait of Robert Johnson is copied from a studio photograph of him taken when he was 25 years of age.

The guitarist writes the cover notes and cites Robert

Johnson as the keystone to his musical foundation and a landmark from which to navigate.

It is June 1st 2007. The fourteen-year-old boy from Newcastle, who turned up at The Pontiac Club all those years ago, is fifty-six years of age and writes an article on the mythology of Robert Johnson.

Robert Johnson and the guitarist move into music's history.

Who knows what last fair deal goes down?

Acknowledgements

'Last Fair Deal Gone Down' first appeared in *Fulcrum* No. 6 USA

Gonna take a little time / Time to think things over...

'I Want To Know What Love Is' by Foreigner

Rocks is my pillows, Stones is my bed ...

'Born and Living With The Blues'
by Sonny Terry & Brownie McGhee & Willie Dixon

A woman is like a dresser
Some men always running thro
Its drawers

'From Four Until Late' by Robert Johnson

Got to keep movin
Got to keep movin
Blues fallin down like hail

Got to keep movin
Got to keep movin
Hellhound on my trail

'Hellhound On My Trail' by Robert Johnson

A NOTE ON THE TYPE

The text of this book is set in Agmena Pro,
Jovica Veljović's Antiqua-influenced
contemporary typeface. A fine choice
for traditional book typography, this beautiful
serif face is nonetheless available in
four different weights for a variety of uses
and was awarded a Certificate
of Excellence at the Type Directors Club
of New York TDC2 competition in 2013.